A Cat's Day

Luke had a very busy day planned.
He ate his breakfast quickly.
He didn't want to be late.

His old cat, Lucy, was
napping in the sun, as usual.

"What a lazy cat!"
Luke thought. But he
loved her anyway.

3

After breakfast, Luke got
ready to go to school.

"Don't forget to do those jobs for me after school!" his mother called out.

"I won't forget, Mum!" Luke promised. "See you later!"

At school, Luke's teacher taught his class all about lions and tigers.

6

Luke could hardly believe that his Lucy was related to such fierce animals!

She was just too lazy!

After school, Luke
stopped at the shops to
pick up some things for
his mother.

The supermarket assistant was very cross. Someone had made a mess in the pet food aisle. "I wonder who did that?" Luke thought.

Next Luke stopped at the pet shop to buy a new collar for Lucy.

"Maybe Lucy would like this ball," he thought.

"Nah, she's much too lazy for a toy like this!" he decided.

Around the corner from his home Luke saw his friend Sally in the clothes shop.

"This shop looks a bit messy today," Luke said to Sally. Sally agreed.

"Well, must get home. Have fun shopping!" said Luke.

When Luke got home, he put down his bags.

He had a lot of homework to do tonight. He was going to write about tigers.

Luke noticed Lucy napping in her usual spot. She gave a quiet yawn. "How can that cat be tired?" he wondered. "She hasn't moved all day!"

Lucy looked up at Luke and yawned. She was tired from her day.

"He'll never know about my adventures," she thought happily.

"He'll never know about my busy day," Lucy thought.

She settled back down in her favourite sunny spot.

Lucy got home just in time!
Boy was just walking in the door.

"This sock will be
a great new toy!"
she thought.

Then Lucy heard a familiar
voice. It was Boy!

"I should get home!"
Lucy thought.

Next, Lucy slipped into the clothes shop. She leapt into a basket of soft socks.

Lucy chased a toy mouse.
"Don't mind me, little
mouse," she miaowed.

11

Lucy visited the pet shop next. It was always full of toys, treats and fish!

"Yum! Delicious cat food!" she purred.

Then Lucy spotted an angry-looking shop assistant, "Uh oh," Lucy thought. "Better get out of here!

Soon Lucy decided it was time for a snack. "I'm getting hungry!" she thought.

Luckily, she wasn't far from the supermarket. Lucy crept inside and tucked in.

8

"These squirrels can really move!"
Lucy thought to herself as she leapt after a
squirrel with a bushy tail.

Lucy's first stop was her favourite tree.
It was always full of squirrels to chase.

"Silly Boy," Lucy thought. "He never notices when I leave!"

5

As soon as Lucy was sure Boy
had left for school, she leapt out
of the window.

4

"What a beautiful morning," Lucy the cat thought.

"I think I'll have an adventure today!"

3